A Rookie reader®

Written by Dana Meachen Rau

Illustrated by Mike Cressy

Children's Press®
A Division of Scholastic Inc.
New York • Toronto • London • Auckland • Sydney
Mexico City • New Delhi • Hong Kong
Danbury, Connecticut

JEAB
R
B R

For Charlie
—D.M.R.

To my one and only purple sister, Cookie
—M.C.

Reading Consultants
Linda Cornwell
Coordinator of School Quality and Professional Improvement
(Indiana State Teachers Association)

Katharine A. Kane
Education Consultant
(Retired, San Diego County Office of Education
and San Diego State University)

Library of Congress Cataloging-in-Publication Data
Rau, Dana Meachen.
    Purple is best/ written by Dana Meachen Rau; illustrated by Mike Cressy.
        p. cm. — (A Rookie reader)
    Summary: Sue's blue paint and Fred's red paint get mixed together and create
purple, the best color of all.
    ISBN 0-516-21638-4 (lib. bdg.)   0-516-27001-X (pbk.)
    [1. Purple—Fiction. 2. Color—Fiction. 3. Painting—Fiction.]
I. Cressy, Mike, ill. II. Title. III. Series.
PZ7.R193975Pu 1999
[E]—dc21   98-53053
                                                   CIP
                                                   AC

© 1999 by Children's Press®, a Division of Grolier Publishing Co., Inc.
Illustration © 1999 by Mike Cressy
Printed in China.
9 10 11 12 13 R 11 10 09 08   62

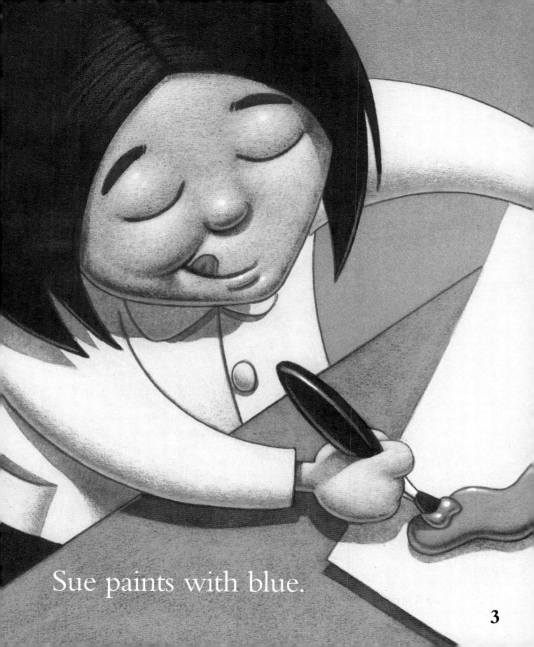

Sue paints with blue.

3

Fred paints
with red.

Sue thinks blue is cool.

8

Fred thinks red is better.

"Try blue," says Sue.

12

"Try red," says Fred.

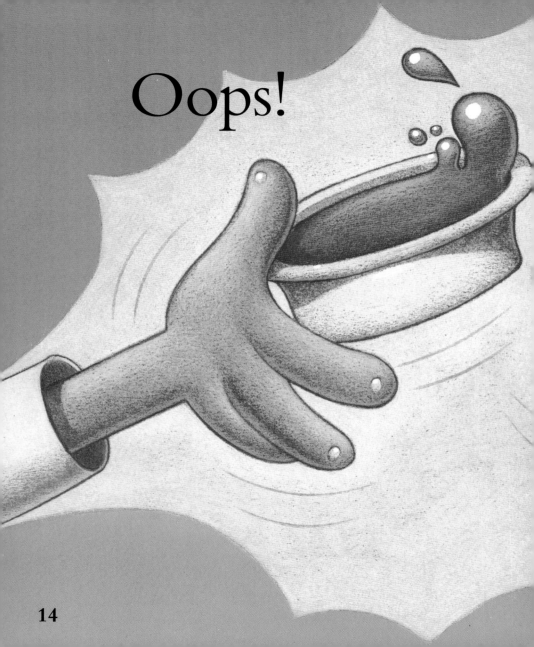

Oops!

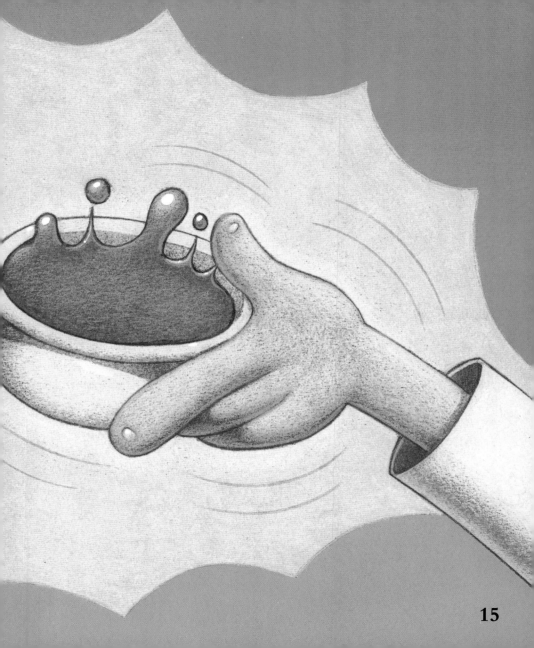

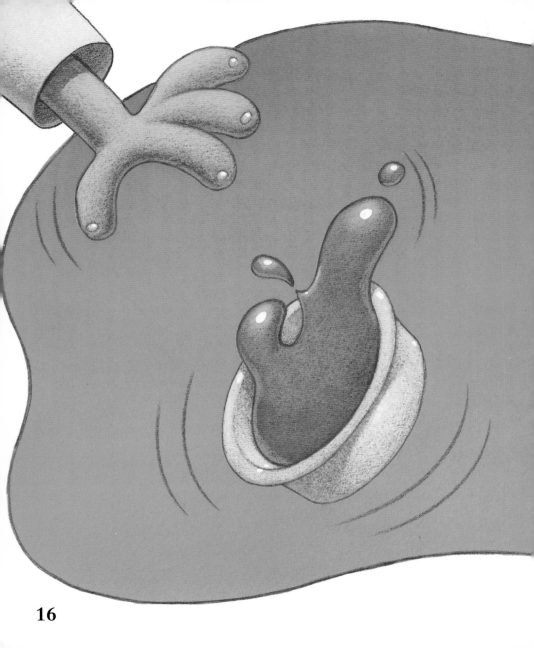

16

The paint
tips and crashes.

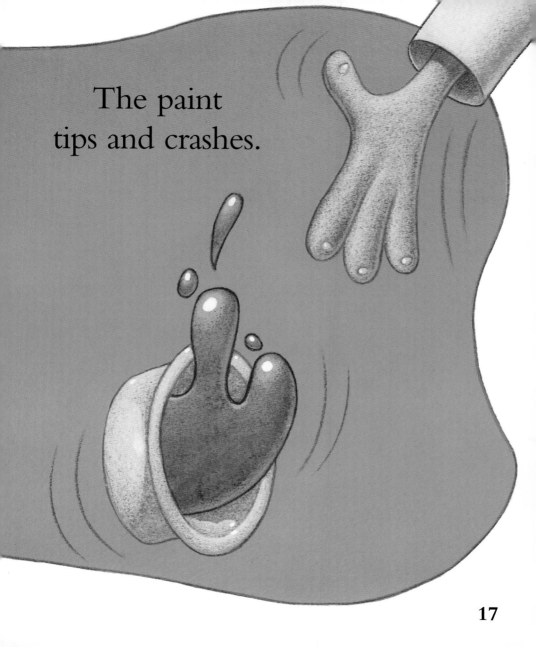

The paint
drips and splashes.

18

Blue mixes with red.

Red mixes with blue.

The pictures
are purple!

"Blue is cool," says Sue.

"Red is better,"
says Fred.

"But purple...

is best!"

WORD LIST (26 words)

and	Fred	says
are	is	splashes
best	mixes	Sue
better	oops	the
blue	paint	thinks
but	paints	tips
cool	pictures	try
crashes	purple	with
drips	red	

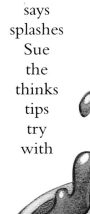

ABOUT THE AUTHOR

Dana Meachen Rau is the author of many books for children, including *A Box Can Be Many Things, The Secret Code,* and *Bob's Vacation* (which she also illustrated) in the Rookie Reader series. She has always studied both writing and art, and loves crafting words and pictures into the perfect story. She also works as a children's book editor and lives with her husband, Chris, and son, Charlie, in Farmington, Connecticut.

ABOUT THE ILLUSTRATOR

Mike Cressy resides in the rainiest part of the United States—Washington State—paints pictures, and tries to stay warm and dry in his hovel, with the help of some hot cocoa.